One Hundred Hundred Days (Plus One)

Add,

For Becky
—M. M.

ISBN 0-439-57462-5

12 11 10 9 8   17 18 19/0

Printed in the U.S.A.   40

First Scholastic printing, January 2004

Book design by Sammy Yuen Jr.

The text for this book was set in CentSchbook BT.

Robin Hill School

One Hundred Days (Plus One)

Written by Margaret McNamara
Illustrated by Mike Gordon

SCHOLASTIC INC.
New York Toronto London Auckland Sydney
Mexico City New Delhi Hong Kong Buenos Aires

Hannah was excited.

Only one week to go
until the party
to celebrate
one hundred days in school.

"That is a long time
to be in school,"
said Hannah.

Mrs. Connor told the class,
"Next Friday,
please bring in
100 little things
to share."

Hannah decided
to bring in buttons.

On Monday, Hannah
found 20 white buttons.

On Tuesday she found
57 mixed buttons.

On Wednesday
she found
4 cat buttons,
6 diamond buttons,

and 13 buttons
with no holes.

On Thursday, Hannah
counted her buttons
from 1 to 100.

CHOooo

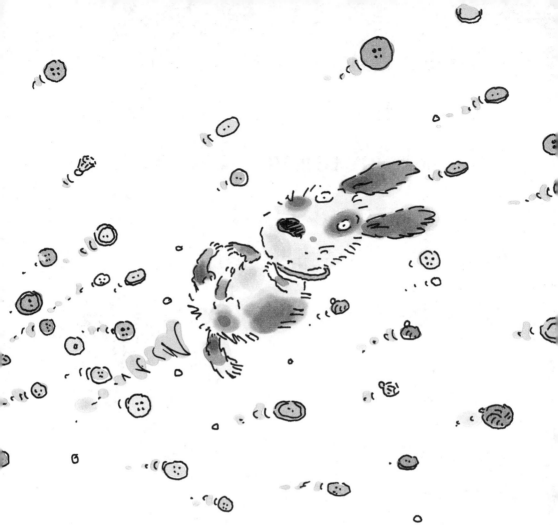

Then she sneezed.

On Friday,
Hannah had a cold.
"No school for you today,"
said her mother.
"On Monday you will
feel better."

On Monday I will feel
worse, thought Hannah.

The party is today.
And I am not there.

On Monday, Hannah's cold
was gone.

She wore her favorite
sweater to school.
It had one big orange button.

Hannah remembered
the 100 buttons.

She had put them
in her backpack,
even though she had
missed the party.

When the school bell rang,
Mrs. Connor said,
"Today is a special day.
What is one hundred
plus one?"

Hannah knew the answer.
"One hundred and one!"
she said.

"Right!" said Mrs. Connor.

"Today we have been in school
for one hundred and one days."
Hannah's friends were smiling.

They showed
101 grains of rice,

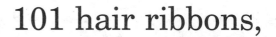

101 hair ribbons,

and 101 postcards.

"I only brought in
100 buttons,"
said Hannah.

"I did not think
to bring in one more,"
she said.

She remembered the button
on her sweater.
"Here is my plus one!"
she said.

"I thought one hundred days
was a long time
to go to school,"
said Hannah.

"And now I have gone
for one hundred plus one!"